Playful Bunny

by Kimberly Zarins

illustrated by Bernadette Pons

Cartwheel
B·O·O·K·S ®

SCHOLASTIC INC.
New York Toronto London Auckland Sydney
Mexico City New Delhi Hong Kong Buenos Aires

The summer day was hot and sunny, but no one wanted to play with Bunny.

Grumpy Hare said,
"Who'd play with a little
ball of fuzz?"

Bunny said, "I'll bet someone does."

From the bank he saw
frogs on lily pads.

"I can hop, too! Wait, stop!"
Bunny tried to follow...
and went plop.

As he scrambled out,
he saw a school of fish,
twirling their tails near him.

But Bunny couldn't swim.

He asked the beavers to play.

"Come join us—there's plenty
of bark to bite."

Bunny tried, but it didn't taste right.

He heard birds
twittering in their nest,
having a grand old time.

But Bunny couldn't climb.

He found some goslings.
They all began to play,

until the mother goose hissed
and chased Bunny away.

In the barn
Bunny found a
kitten with some yarn.

"Let's play together,
no need to play alone!"

He saw a cow getting milked.
The pail was frothy-fizzy.

"Will you play with me, please?" Bunny asked.

Said the cow, "I'm a little busy."

It was becoming
a lonely day.

"Doesn't anybody want to play?"

"I will," said a puppy.

They wrestled with
paws and teeth,

But Bunny got squished underneath.

Then they heard a whistle,
and the puppy raced away.

"Come back!" Bunny chased after.
He had to find someone
who would play.

He watched a
boy throw
a stick.

The puppy raced for it double-quick,
but Bunny beat him to the spot.

"Those are fast feet you've got!"

The boy laughed and all
three played, and learned the
things Bunny could do.

Racing, hide-and-seek,
digging, nose-touching...

With perfect ears
for peekaboo,
and a perfect shape
for cuddling, too.